My
Pregnancy
Journal

ANNE GEDDES

My Pregnancy Journal

ANNE GEDDES

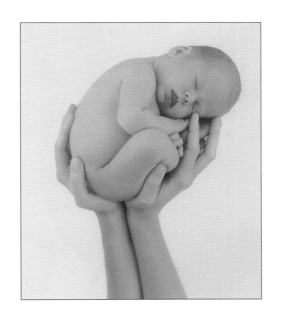

My Pregnancy Journal

by

Finding Out

Finding Out

Baby's due date _____

_____

_____

I thought I might be pregnant because _____

_____

_____

_____

_____

_____

_____

_____

_____

_____

_____

_____

_____

Finding Out

How I felt when the pregnancy was confirmed _____

_____

_____

_____

_____

_____

_____

_____

Who was with me at the time _____

_____

_____

_____

_____

_____

_____

_____

_____

Finding Out

Who I shared the news with first . . . Their reaction _____

Finding Out

Reaction of family and friends to the news _____

_____

_____

_____

_____

_____

_____

_____

_____

_____

_____

_____

_____

_____

_____

_____

First Things First

Where I would like to give birth _____

_____

_____

_____

_____

_____

_____

I chose _____ *as my caregiver because* _____

_____

_____

_____

_____

_____

_____

_____

_____

Feelings About Becoming a Mother

My thoughts on motherhood _____

_____

_____

_____

_____

_____

_____

_____

My thoughts on childhood _____

_____

_____

_____

_____

_____

_____

_____

_____

_____

Journey Through Pregnancy

the first
three months

Journey Through Pregnancy

Changes I have noticed about my body _____

Journey Through Pregnancy

My food preferences _____

_____

_____

_____

_____

_____

_____

Foods and drinks I cannot tolerate _____

_____

_____

_____

_____

_____

_____

_____

_____

Journey Through Pregnancy

I am excited about _____

_____

_____

_____

_____

_____

_____

_____

_____

_____

_____

_____

_____

_____

_____

_____

Journey Through Pregnancy

I am feeling anxious about _____

Good Advice

Interesting things I have learned or been told by others _____

_____

_____

_____

_____

_____

_____

_____

Some good advice I received from _____ *was* _____

_____

_____

_____

_____

_____

_____

_____

_____

My Disappearing Waistline

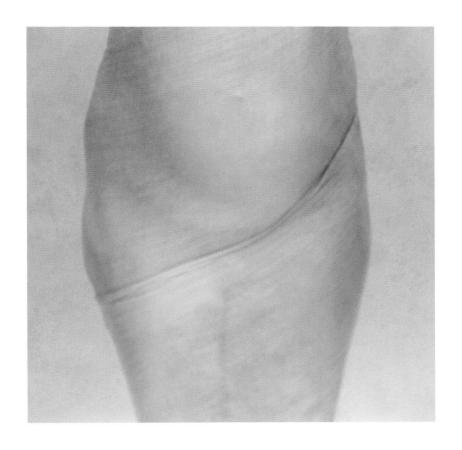

the second three months

My Disappearing Waistline

What I am really enjoying about being pregnant _____

_____

_____

_____

_____

_____

_____

_____

_____

But this isn't much fun _____

_____

_____

_____

_____

_____

My Disappearing Waistline

Changes I have noticed about my body _____

First Look

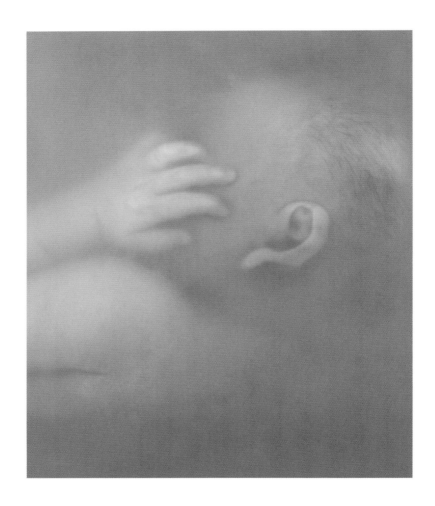

My first ultrasound was at _____

_____

_____

How I felt about the ultrasound _____

_____

_____

_____

_____

_____

_____

_____

_____

_____

_____

_____

_____

First Look

I wanted to know the sex of my baby because _____

_____

_____

_____

_____

_____

_____

_____

_____

_____

_____

_____

_____

_____

_____

_____

_____

_____

First Look

I did not want to know the sex of my baby because _____

_____

_____

_____

_____

_____

_____

_____

_____

_____

_____

_____

_____

_____

_____

A Special Note to My Baby

I have been thinking about _____

_____

_____

_____

_____

_____

_____

_____

I would like you to know _____

_____

_____

_____

_____

_____

_____

_____

_____

_____

Baby's First Movements

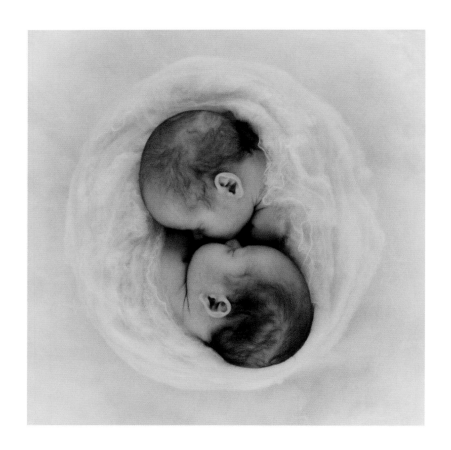

I first felt my baby move _____

_____

_____

It felt like _____

_____

_____

_____

_____

_____

How long it was before someone else could feel my baby move _____

_____

_____

_____

_____

_____

_____

_____

What's Ahead

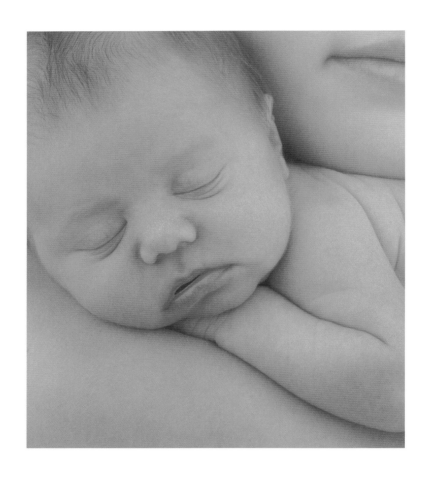

I am attending childbirth classes at _____

_____

_____

_____

Useful information _____

_____

_____

_____

_____

_____

_____

_____

_____

_____

_____

_____

_____

_____

_____

Keeping Up

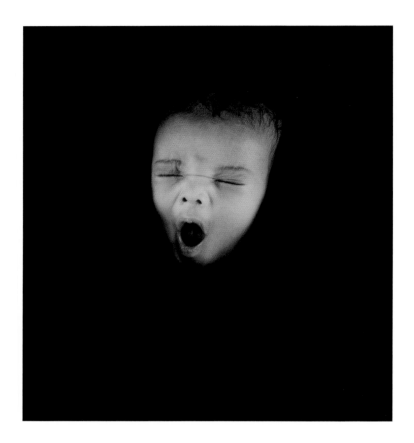

Comments about my visits to my caregiver _____

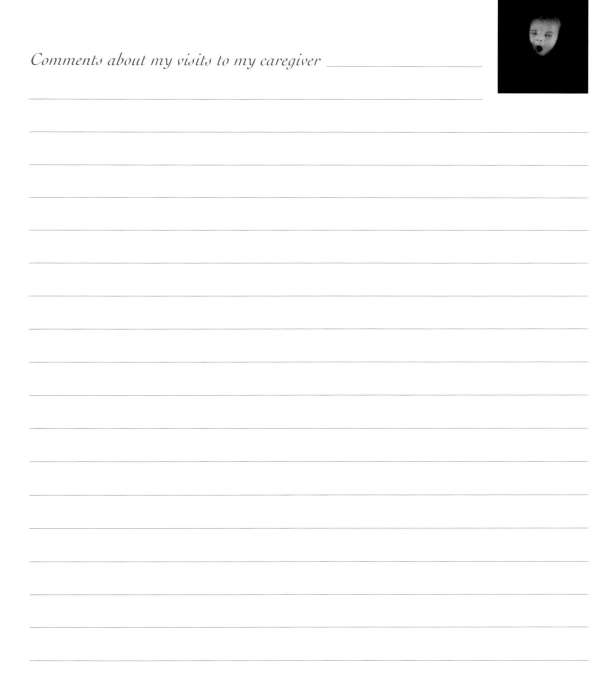

Changing Relationships

How being pregnant has changed my relationship with those close to me

Changing Relationships

How being pregnant is different from what I expected _____

_____

_____

_____

_____

_____

_____

_____

_____

_____

_____

_____

_____

_____

_____

_____

_____

_____

Changing Relationships

How I am feeling about myself and being pregnant _____

_____

_____

_____

_____

_____

_____

_____

_____

_____

_____

_____

_____

_____

_____

_____

_____

Special Moments

Things I most enjoy doing for myself _____

_____

_____

_____

_____

_____

_____

I take time for myself by _____

_____

_____

_____

_____

_____

_____

_____

_____

Hopes and Dreams

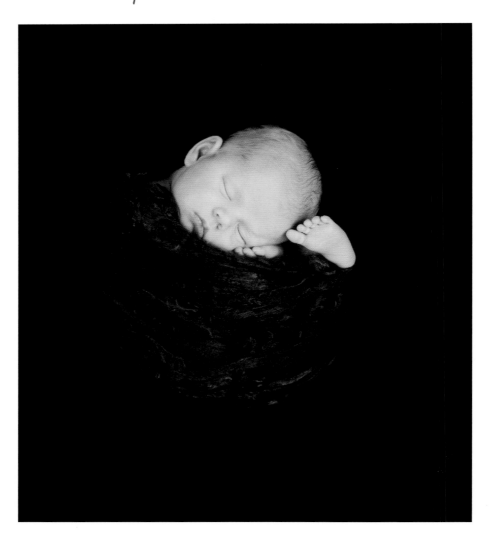

What I most wish for my baby _____

The Home Stretch

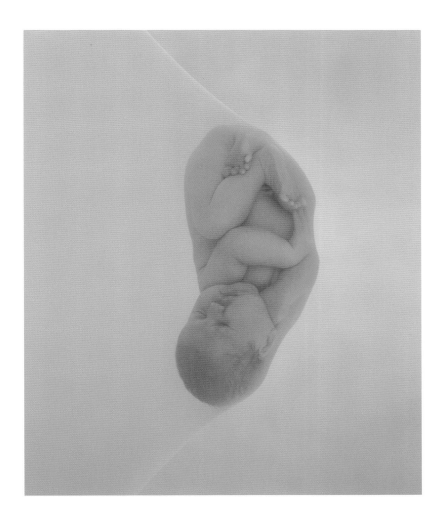

the last
three months

The Home Stretch

What I am really enjoying about being pregnant _____

_____

_____

_____

_____

_____

_____

_____

_____

But this isn't much fun _____

_____

_____

_____

_____

_____

The Home Stretch

Changes I have noticed about my body _____

_____

_____

_____

_____

_____

_____

_____

_____

_____

_____

_____

_____

_____

_____

_____

_____

_____

_____

The Home Stretch

I am excited about _____

_____

_____

_____

_____

_____

_____

I am feeling anxious about _____

_____

_____

_____

_____

_____

_____

_____

_____

The Home Stretch

Dreams I have been having _____

_____

_____

_____

_____

_____

_____

What I think they might mean _____

_____

_____

_____

_____

_____

_____

About My Baby

My baby is most active _____

About My Baby

My baby seems to respond to _____

_____

_____

_____

_____

_____

_____

_____

_____

_____

_____

_____

_____

_____

_____

_____

_____

About My Baby

Special things I enjoy doing for my baby _____

This Time

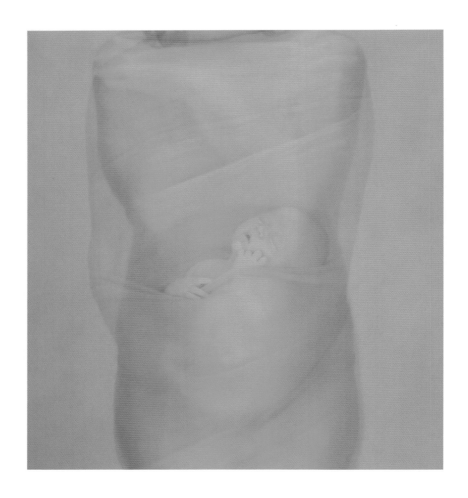

I feel being pregnant this time is either different, or the same, because

Names

Names I am thinking about for my baby:

Boys _____

_____

_____

_____

_____

Girls _____

_____

_____

_____

_____

Pet names I have for my baby _____

_____

_____

_____

_____

Best Guesses

People's comments regarding the likely sex of the baby _____

_____

_____

_____

_____

_____

_____

_____

My own feelings about the sex of my baby _____

_____

_____

_____

_____

_____

_____

_____

_____

For the Baby

Special things I have for this baby _____

Gifts I Have Received

Gifts I have received: _____

_____

_____

_____

_____

_____

_____

_____

_____

_____

_____

_____

_____

_____

_____

_____

_____

_____

Favorite Clothes

My favorite piece of clothing is _____

_____

_____

Because _____

_____

_____

_____

_____

_____

_____

_____

_____

_____

_____

Looking Back

The best thing about being pregnant has been _____

Looking Back

The worst thing about being pregnant has been _____

_____

_____

_____

_____

_____

_____

_____

_____

_____

_____

_____

_____

_____

_____

_____

_____

Looking Back

Being pregnant has taught me _____

_____

_____

_____

_____

_____

_____

_____

_____

_____

I have had great support from _____

_____

_____

_____

_____

Looking Forward

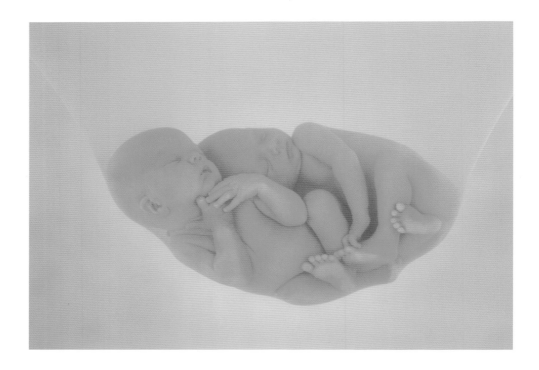

My thoughts about giving birth _____

Looking Forward

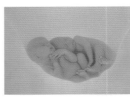

Who I want to support me at the birth _____

_____

_____

_____

_____

_____

_____

Who else I would like to be with me to share the experience _____

_____

_____

_____

_____

_____

_____

_____

Looking Forward

I am excited about _____

_____

_____

_____

_____

_____

_____

I feel anxious about _____

_____

_____

_____

_____

_____

_____

_____

Another Special Note to My Baby

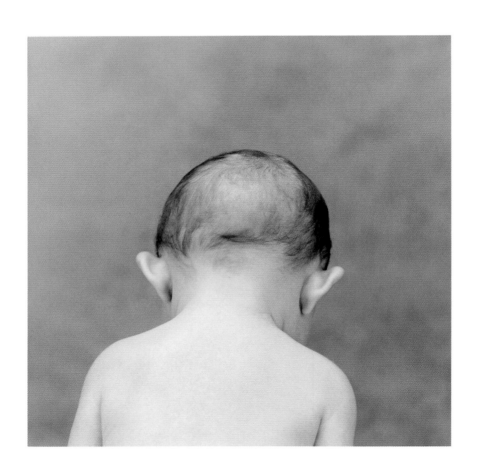

I have been thinking about _____

_____

_____

_____

_____

_____

_____

_____

I would like you to know _____

_____

_____

_____

_____

_____

_____

_____

Bits and Pieces

Special things I would like to have with me at the birth:

The Birth of My Baby

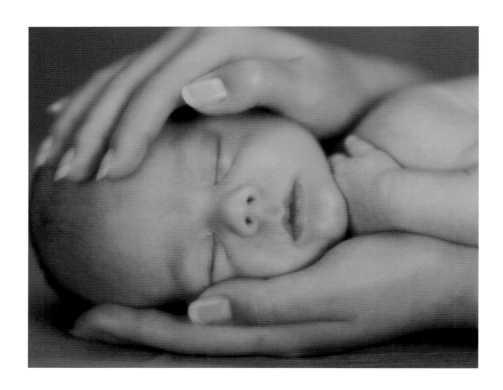

I knew I was in labor because _____

_____

_____

_____

_____

_____

_____

Where I was _____

_____

_____

Date and time _____

_____

_____

_____

The Birth

Who was with me at the birth _____

_____

_____

_____

_____

_____

_____

_____

_____

_____

_____

_____

_____

_____

_____

_____

_____

The Birth

Comments about the labor _____

_____

_____

_____

_____

_____

_____

_____

_____

_____

_____

_____

_____

_____

_____

_____

_____

_____

_____

First Impressions

Who cried first _____

_____

_____

_____

_____

My first words to my baby _____

_____

_____

_____

_____

_____

_____

_____

_____

_____

_____

_____

_____

First Impressions

My first thoughts and feelings when my baby was born _____

_____

_____

_____

_____

_____

_____

_____

_____

Who my baby most looks like _____

_____

_____

_____

_____

First Impressions

My biggest surprise about giving birth _____

A Special Note to Me

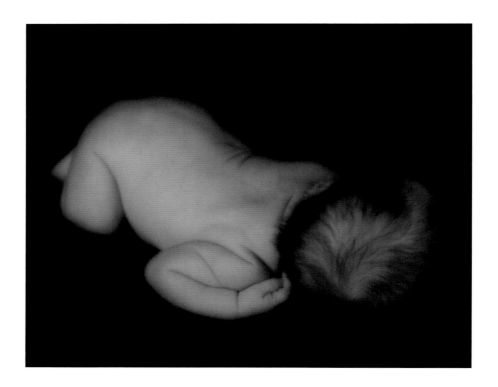

I feel really proud of myself because _____

Just Me

The best thing about not being pregnant is _____

_____

_____

_____

_____

_____

_____

_____

The thing I miss about being pregnant is _____

_____

_____

_____

_____

_____

_____

_____

_____

A Note to Others

The single best piece of advice I could give to other pregnant women:

ANNE GEDDES ®

www.annegeddes.com

© 2003 Anne Geddes

The right of Anne Geddes to be identified as the Author of the
Work has been asserted by her in accordance with the
Copyright, Designs and Patents Act 1988.

First published in 2003 by Photogenique Publishers
(a division of Hodder Moa Beckett)
4 Whetu Place, Mairangi Bay, Auckland, New Zealand

This edition published in North America in 2004 by
Andrews McMeel Publishing
4520 Main Street, Kansas City, MO 64111-7701

Produced by Kel Geddes
Printed in China by Midas Printing Ltd, Hong Kong

ISBN 0-7407-4392-9

04 05 06 MID 10 9 8 7 6 5 4 3 2 1